MW01113494

LIFE IN ANCIENT ROME

Illustrations by
John Green

Introduction and text by
William Kaufman

DOVER PUBLICATIONS, INC.
Mineola, New York

Bibliographical Note

Life in Ancient Rome is a new work, first published by Dover Publications, Inc., in 1997.

DOVER *Pictorial Archive* SERIES

International Standard Book Number: 0-486-29767-5

Manufactured in the United States of America
Dover Publications, Inc., 31 East 2nd Street, Mineola, N.Y. 11501

INTRODUCTION

The Roman Way

According to an old Latin proverb, "All roads lead to Rome"—not only the remarkable network of highways the Romans built to tie together the vast reaches of their ancient empire, but also the roads of language, culture, and history: if we trace back in time the paths of our alphabet and much of our vocabulary, our political institutions and laws, our architecture, our theater, our sports—in short, much of who we are as a people and a civilization—we find ourselves smack in the center of ancient Rome, "the mother of men."

Following many of these same roads farther back in time would lead us to another great city-state, ancient Athens, which the Romans freely acknowledged as their mentor in religion, art, and philosophy. Most of the educated citizens of ancient Rome studied Greek and viewed classical Athenian civilization as a spiritual ideal. But the distinctive genius of Rome was more worldly than spiritual. The awesome imperial march of the Roman armies created the greatest domain of political power in Western history, extending, at its height in A.D. 117, from Scotland to Arabia and from the Straits of Gibraltar to the Black Sea and spanning, in one form or another, nearly two thousand years.

The price of such worldly glory was steep. The roads from Rome are strewn not only with cultural monuments and technological marvels (some Roman bridges and aqueducts are still functioning throughout Europe today) but also with signposts of brutality, cruelty, and exploitation: the same Roman highways that spread luminous words like *republic* and *virtue* also left a trail of ignoble names like *gladiator* and *dictator*. In spite of—perhaps because of—these contradictions, the sheer magnitude and grandeur of Rome's rise and fall still inspire awe and fascination.

Historical Background

Originating as a small Etruscan settlement of a few thousand in the eighth century B.C., Rome made the transition to republican rule early in the fifth century B.C.; by the third century B.C. the city was a major power in the Mediterranean, poised to vanquish its major rival, Carthage, and to expand into Macedonia, Greece, and Spain during the middle republic

(264–133 B.C.). During the following century republican rule broke down amidst internal dissension that erupted into civil war between rival Roman generals; the victor, Julius Caesar, emerged as the unchallenged dictator of Rome in 46 B.C. but was assassinated two years later. The ensuing civil conflict ended when Mark Antony was defeated at Actium in 31 B.C. by Octavian, Caesar's adopted son, who ruled as Augustus from 27 B.C. to A.D. 14, inaugurating a 200-year period of peace in the Mediterranean world known as *pax Romana,* the Roman peace.

Internal political strife persisted within Rome, however, following the suicide of the last Augustan emperor, Nero, in A.D. 68. His successor, Vespasian, inaugurated the Flavian dynasty, which was followed by the Antonines until A.D. 192. During this period the Roman Empire stretched to its greatest expanse, in 117 under Trajan.

The Severi Dynasty (A.D. 193–235) was followed by an unstable period until the ascension of the "Illyrian" emperors (270–284). Diocletian's reign (284–305) restored centralized authority for a time, but pressures from European tribes and from internal conflicts took a progressive toll on Roman authority, leading to a division of the empire into more manageable eastern and western halves in A.D. 395, with the eastern capital located in Constantinople.

During the fifth century the European tribes made further inroads into the Western Empire, culminating in the sack of Rome by the Visigoths in A.D. 410. The final western emperor, Romulus Augustulus, was overthrown in A.D. 476, while the Eastern (Byzantine) Empire endured until the Turkish conquest of Constantinople in A.D. 1453.

A Note to the Reader

The vivid, detailed drawings in this book immerse the reader in the Roman Empire at its peak, joining historical highlights with a variety of scenes from the social, political, cultural, and religious life of ancient Rome. The book can serve as an illustrated supplement to a classroom text or simply as a coloring book for self-guided study or recreation. Whatever the application, we hope that somewhere amidst these pictures and words you or your students will find a road to "the grandeur that was Rome."

CONTENTS

Marius defeats the Germanic invaders at Aquae Sextiae (Aix-en-Provence), 102 B.C. Gaius Marius, born to the middle class, was a major politician and army officer in the late years of the Roman Republic. After an important military victory in Africa, he went on to halt a major threat to Italy from German tribes, routing them at Aquae Sextiae (Aix-en-Provence) in 102 B.C. He served seven one-year terms as consul, the chief officer of the republican government. After commanding a force in the Social War of 90–89 B.C., he unsuccessfully opposed Sulla for command of the Asian armed forces. He died in 86 B.C.

Sulla named dictator, 82 B.C. Lucius Sulla came from an aristocratic family and early on showed a flair for politics and warfare, distinguishing himself in the war in Africa, serving as a *praetor* (one of the chief magistrates) in 94 B.C., and fighting in the Social War of 90–89 B.C. Elected one of two consuls in 88 B.C., he was appointed to lead his army against King Mithradates in Pontus in Asia Minor. When the command was suddenly transferred to Marius, Sulla rallied forces loyal to him and marched on Rome, killing and exiling his opponents.

After defeating Mithradates and conquering Greece, Sulla again marched on Rome (where he had been declared a public enemy by the antiaristocratic party), entering the city in 82 B.C., when he was appointed dictator. He then launched a reign of terror against his political opponents. After ushering in a series of political reforms aimed at shoring up the central government by strengthening the Senate, he stepped down as dictator in 80 B.C. He died two years later.

5

The "triumph" (victory parade) of Pompey after his African campaign, 80 B.C. The triumph, the highest honor a general could receive in ancient Rome, was an elaborate parade held to celebrate a major military victory, complete with trumpeters, sacrificial animals, marching soldiers, displays of booty and prisoners of war, and the presentation of a laurel or palm to Jupiter at the Capitoline temple. The triumph in the picture was the first of three for the aristocratic general and politician Pompey: in 80 for his defeat of the pro-Marius forces in Africa;

in 70 for his victories in Spain; and, in 61, the greatest of all for his eastern campaigns. A major power by that time, he teamed up with Caesar and Crassus in 59 to form the First Triumvirate, a secret agreement to share power among the three. Personal and political conflicts soon splintered the alliance, and Caesar's armies defeated those of Pompey, who was murdered while in exile in Egypt in 48 B.C.

Crassus puts down the slave revolt led by Spartacus, 71 B.C. The most disturbing blight on Roman civilization was slavery. Historians estimate that by 100 B.C. there were some four hundred thousand slaves in Rome, roughly one third of the population. Humane attitudes toward slaves became more common by the end of the second century B.C.: some household slaves were treated with familial regard and affection, and many slave owners arranged to free their slaves in their wills; other slaves purchased their freedom for an amount equivalent to their market value. In time there was a substantial population of such freedmen in Rome. Earlier in Roman history, however, the slave population—drawn chiefly from prisoners of war—was often subject to brutal treatment, including forced participation in gladiatorial contests.

One such slave, Spartacus, was a Thracian deserter from the Roman army who was forced into gladiatorial training at Padua. He fled with some comrades in 73 B.C. and was joined by other runaway slaves on Mount Vesuvius. Gathering a force that eventually numbered ninety thousand, Spartacus occupied much of southern Italy but was finally defeated and killed in 71 by Roman legions under the command of Marcus Licinius Crassus, who crucified six thousand of the rebels. Crassus went on to form the First Triumvirate with Caesar and Pompey; Spartacus's name became a rallying symbol for subsequent revolutionary movements in Western history.

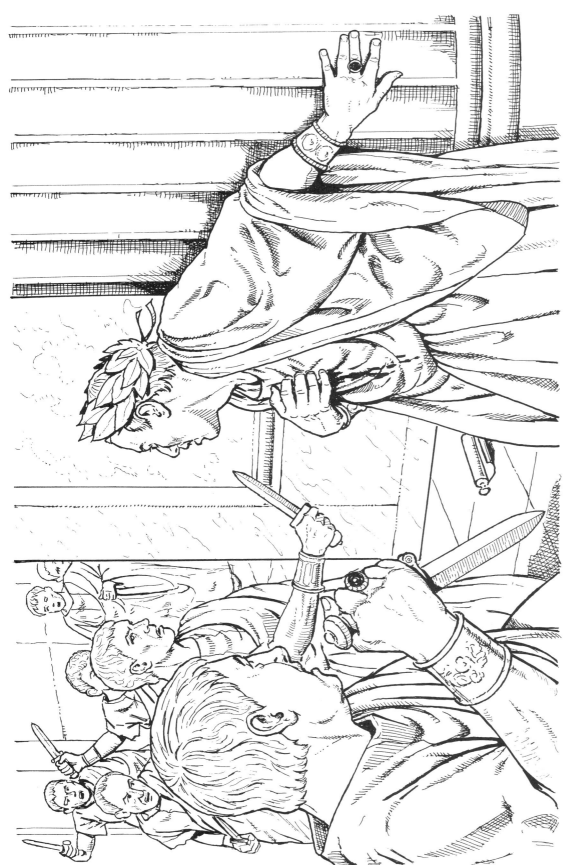

The Assassination of Julius Caesar, 44 B.C. The name Julius Caesar still rings out across the centuries, summoning images of power, ruthlessness, majesty, and tragedy. He claimed divine descent but was born to an undistinguished aristocratic family in 100 B.C. Starting out as a young prosecutor, Caesar served stints of routine military service during his swift rise through a series of minor political offices, finally emerging into prominence with his election as *pontifex maximus* (ceremonial head of state clergy) in 63 and *praetor* (high judge) in 62. He displayed formidable administrative and military talents during his term as governor of Farther Spain (61–60) and upon returning to Rome in 59 parlayed his growing power into election as consul (head of state) and cofounder of the First Triumvirate with Crassus and Pompey.

Caesar's armies vanquished Gaul over the next nine years, but he found his triumphant return to Rome blocked by his jealous rival, Pompey. In the ensuing civil war, Caesar routed Pompey in 48 and then led successful campaigns in Egypt, Pontus, and North Africa. Greeted in Rome in 45 by a triumph of unrivaled splendor, he assumed unprecedented powers in challenging the entrenched aristocrats of the Senate; soon after the Senate declared him "dictator for life" in 44, sixty senators, alarmed at the vast extent of his power, surrounded him as he entered the Senate on March 15, 44, the Ides of March, and stabbed him to death.

Cicero attacks the character of Mark Antony before the Senate, 43 B.C.
Originally an advisory body to the early Roman kings, the Senate evolved into the most powerful part of the government in the Roman Republic. Its three hundred members, appointed to life terms by the censors, came from the Republic's leading families and exercised considerable influence over legislation, finances, and foreign policy.

As the Senate's power grew, oratory became an increasingly valuable weapon in shaping its decisions, and no one wielded it with greater mastery than Cicero (106–43 B.C.), a statesman, writer, and advocate whose speeches and writings eloquently upheld the traditional republican principles that were in retreat from the assaults of civil war and imperial ambition.

Having established a reputation for eloquence while representing clients in the courts, Cicero turned to politics, where he rose rapidly through the ranks, attaining the consulship in 63. Exiled in 58 for having vehemently denounced the First Triumvirate as unconstitutional, he was recalled in 57 through the intercession of his ally Pompey and resigned himself to the triumvirate.

During the scramble to succeed the slain Caesar, Cicero delivered a series of speeches (Philippics) to the Senate in 43 B.C., inveighing against Mark Antony and warning of his dictatorial aspirations. When, later that year, Antony joined with his chief rivals, Octavian and Lepidus, to form the Second Triumvirate (see page 11), they marked Cicero for execution; after he was captured and killed on December 3, 43, his head and hands were displayed on the speakers' platform in the Forum in Rome as a warning to other potential dissenters.

Augustus (Octavian) (reigned 27 B.C.–A.D. 14) at the dedication of the *Ara Pacis* (Altar of Peace), 9 B.C. When the eighteen-year-old Octavian returned to Rome in 44 B.C., he learned that his great-uncle, Julius Caesar, had adopted him and left him the bulk of his vast estate. Determined to stake his claim to power, he faced a formidable rival in Mark Antony. Soon Antony, Octavian, and Lepidus, a minor partner, formed the Second Triumvirate on November 27, 43. Over the next several years Antony and Octavian routed the remaining republican opposition and, brushing Lepidus aside, divided the provinces between them, Antony controlling the East and Octavian the West.

By 32 Antony, having fallen under the spell of Cleopatra, was on a collision course with Octavian, who defeated Antony in a naval clash at Actium, Greece,

in 31; the fleeing Antony and Cleopatra committed suicide the following year.

Now, in his own words, "master of all things," Octavian applied his administrative genius to taming the fractious Roman state: trimming the size of the unruly Senate and stacking it with his supporters, he expanded his authority, first as consul and later under the new titles *princeps civitatis* ("first citizen") and, most notably and enduringly, *augustus* ("worshipful"). In consolidating his personal power, Augustus became the first true Roman emperor and achieved the stability that allowed the Empire to thrive in peace (*pax Romana*) for the following two hundred years. The magnitude of his achievement was recognized midway through his forty-one-year reign, when the Senate dedicated the *Ara Pacis*, "altar of peace," in his honor in 9 B.C.

11

Tiberius (reigned A.D. 14–37) at his villa on Capri. Tiberius (42 B.C.–A.D. 37) became Augustus's stepson in 38 B.C., when Augustus, dazzled by the beauty of Tiberius's mother, Livia, commanded her to divorce her husband and become the emperor's wife. After receiving a rigorous education in the royal household, Tiberius showed his mettle as a leader in successful military campaigns in Parthia, Germany, and Pannonia. After reluctantly acceding to Augustus's order to divorce his beloved wife, Vipsania, to marry the emperor's widowed daughter, Julia, the intensely aggrieved Tiberius suddenly sought and received permission to retire to the island of Rhodes to devote himself to study and reflection while the frolicsome Julia tormented him with her very public infidelities back in Rome. During these four years of exile, the once-dutiful soldier and family man seems to have evolved into a cruel, self-indulgent voluptuary.

After the death of his two older sons, Augustus adopted Tiberius, who ascended to the throne upon the emperor's death in A.D. 14. Tiberius proved himself an honest and productive administrator but at length grew weary of public life and retreated to his elaborate villas on the island of Capri, delegating day-to-day authority to his chief associate, Sejeanus. While on Capri the increasingly isolated and eccentric emperor indulged his growing taste for bizarre and sadistic entertainments, including (by some accounts) savoring the sight of his enemies being thrown from cliffs. By the time of his death in A.D. 37, Tiberius was a remote and despised figure in the city he had once served so ably.

Caligula (reigned A.D. 37–41) demanding to be worshiped as the god Jupiter. Tiberius's only sons—Julius Caesar Drusus and the adopted Germanicus (his nephew)—having died, the aging emperor turned to Germanicus's offspring in search of a successor. He settled on Gaius Caesar (A.D. 12–41), better known to posterity as Caligula, meaning "little boots," a nickname bestowed on him by the troops in his father's army.

At first Caligula seemed to be a ruler of great promise: he suspended the treason trials initiated by Tiberius, granted amnesty to political exiles, reinstituted public accounting of the state treasury, and held games. Then, from this enlightened trajectory he abruptly plunged into an abyss of despotism, cruelty, and perversity. He resumed the treason

trials, plundered the treasury, and set himself up as a god, forming his own priesthood and building a temple featuring a life-size statue of himself made out of pure gold. No one was exempt from his mad whims: not his father-in-law, whom he caused to cut his own throat, nor his sister, with whom he may have had an incestuous relationship. What little beneficence he showed was apt to take bizarre forms, such as conferring the consulship on his horse. His follies extended to foreign policy, including an abortive invasion of Britain and uprisings in Judaea and Alexandria.

There were few mourners after a conspiracy led to Caligula's murder by a tribune of the Praetorian Guard at the Palatine games on January 24, 41.

Claudius (reigned A.D. 41–54) personally attends the capture of Camulodunum (Colchester) during the conquest of Britain, A.D. 43. Claudius (10 B.C.–A.D. 54) was Tiberius's nephew and a grandson of Livia Drusilla, Augustus's wife. He was physically infirm but intellectually precocious; his unsteady gait, slurred speech, and unappealing looks were an embarrassment to the imperial family, which was happy to relegate him to his scholarly interest in history. After the murder of Caligula, a soldier found Claudius trembling in the imperial palace; the leaders of the powerful Praetorian Guard (the palace troops), believing they had found a pliant candidate, declared him emperor the following day.

The shy, enfeebled scholar became a forceful, capable ruler. He further centralized political power, in part through creating a cabinet of secretaries composed of freedmen who wielded great authority. He launched a major public

works program and judiciously expanded the empire, annexing client kingdoms such as Mauretania, Lycia, and Thrace and conquering Britain in A.D. 43, a campaign he commanded in person in its final stages.

Despite this solid record of achievement, Claudius's regime fell prey to several major weaknesses. His freedman secretaries became influential and corrupt enough to concern many senators. Unable to resist the temptations of power, the emperor assumed ever greater judicial power, issuing harsh, arbitrary judgments and summarily executing senators and family members.

Claudius's reign came to an abrupt and violent end. Agrippina, his power-mad fourth wife, grew impatient for the succession of her son by a previous marriage—Lucius Domitius Ahenobarbus (later known as Nero)—and poisoned Claudius on October 13, A.D. 54.

Nero (reigned A.D. 54–68) during the great fire in Rome, A.D. 64 In the saga of Nero (A.D. 37–68), imperial narcissism, cruelty, and eccentricity balloon to lurid proportions. He grew up under the long shadow cast by his feverishly ambitious and domineering mother, Agrippina. But thanks to the salutary influence of his tutor Seneca (an eminent philosopher), Nero, in his first five years as emperor, won widespread popularity with his magnanimous and moderate policies.

Public adulation, however, fostered a vanity that quickly transformed the youthful idealist into a murderous despot whose victims included his stepbrother, mother, and wife as well as eighteen political opponents, including Seneca and the poet Lucan.

His epic megalomania was not confined to politics. Convinced that his modest talents as a lyre player and singer marked him as a great artist, he inspired scorn with mediocre public performances; he offended others with his public espousal of eastern mystery religions such as Zoroastrianism.

Contrary to popular legend, Nero was probably not responsible for the fire that left most of Rome a ruin in 64, nor did he fiddle idly while the city smoldered. His vigorous rebuilding program, although admirable in many respects, included construction of a monument to his insatiable ego, the Golden Palace, a monstrosity that would have covered a third of Rome if completed.

Pervasive doubts about Nero's sanity and competence climaxed when he mockingly laughed at reports of revolts by provincial governors in Gaul and Spain; the Senate denounced him and the Praetorian Guard turned against him. His doom sealed, Nero became his own final victim when he committed suicide at age 31.

An eruption of Mount Vesuvius buries Pompeii, A.D. 79. Nero's death marked the end of the Julio-Claudian line of emperors ("the progeny of the Caesars") and set off a civil war among competing commanders from which Vespasian (reigned 69–79), a man of the middle class, emerged victorious. He was effective in restoring peace and stability in the empire and solvency in the treasury.

Having secured the supremacy of his Flavian house, Vespasian designated Titus, his older son, as his successor. Titus (reigned 79–81) faced two major

disasters during his brief reign: another great fire in Rome and the destruction of the seaside towns of Pompeii and Herculaneum during the eruption of Mount Vesuvius in 79.

Sealed against the ravages of time by a blanket of volcanic debris—nineteen to twenty-three feet at Pompeii and sixty-five feet at Herculaneum—these two sites have yielded a trove of precious details about ancient Roman life available nowhere else: streets and sidewalks full of shops, bakeries (with that

morning's bread still in the ovens when discovered nearly two thousand years later!), inns, schools with students' writing tablets, a banker's accounts, graffiti about love and politics, and the lavish villas of the wealthy, which have revealed more about Roman painting, tile art, and mores than any other source—even the local brothel is impeccably preserved, complete with pornographic wall paintings (see pages 36 and 37 for more details about life in Pompeii).

Titus's generous efforts to cope with these disasters earned him great popularity. He was succeeded by his younger brother, Diomitian (reigned 81–96), whose reign was notable for his high-handed treatment of the Senate, which regarded him as a tyrant; with his murder in 96, the Flavian dynasty came to an end.

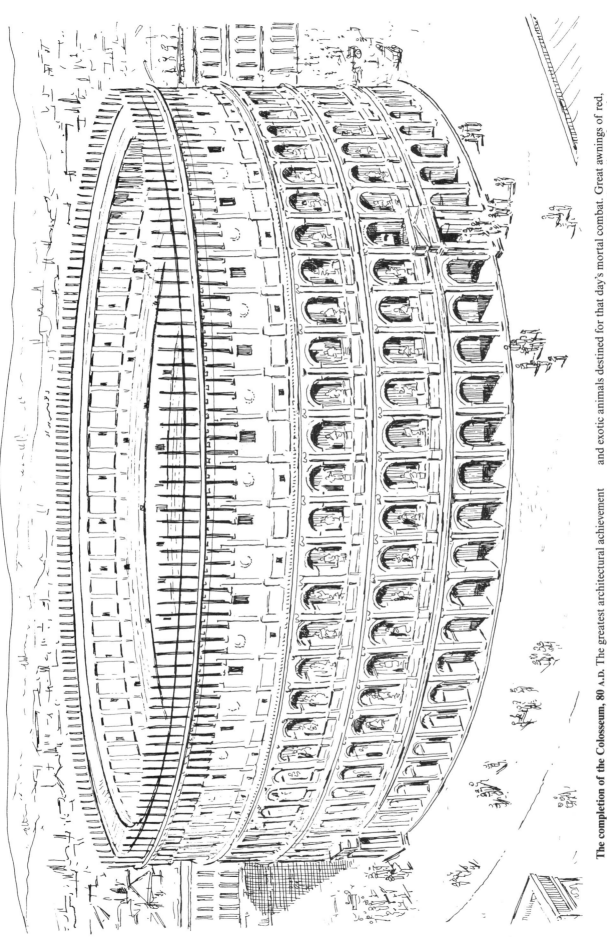

The completion of the Colosseum, 80 A.D. The greatest architectural achievement of the Flavian period—indeed, one of the greatest in Roman history—was the Colosseum, the great amphitheater conceived as far back as the reign of Augustus and finally completed under Titus, in 80. Although preceded by other oval stadiums, the Colosseum (also known as the Flavian Amphitheater) was by far the largest and most magnificent, measuring one third of a mile around with an outer facing that rose four stories to a height of 160 feet.

The interior boasted three tiers—supported by an elaborate network of arches, vaults, and piers—that accommodated crowds of up to fifty thousand. A labyrinth of underground passageways and trap doors concealed the gladiators

and exotic animals destined for that day's mortal combat. Great awnings of red, yellow, and blue billowed above the stadium, shielding the audience from the glare of the sun and imparting an eerie hue to the bloody spectacle unfolding in the arena (see page 45 for more on gladiatorial combats).

Although restored under later emperors, the Colosseum was subsequently damaged by earthquakes and fell into disrepair by the Middle Ages, serving chiefly as a source of building materials for pillagers until Pope Pius VIII (reigned 1829–30) launched a preservation effort. Every day thousands of tourists still flock to the crumbling remains of this once-proud monument to the glory—and brutality—of Roman civilization.

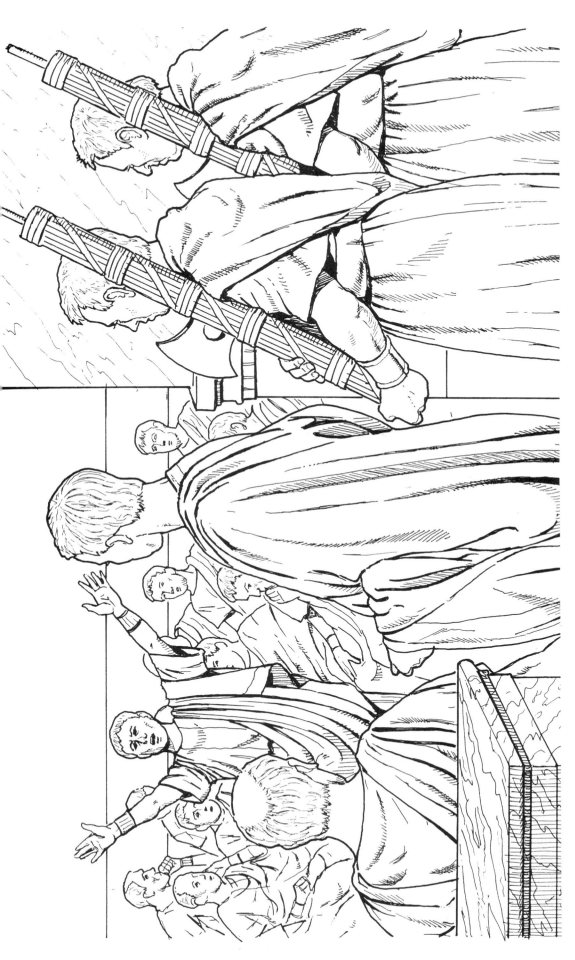

The two consuls, attended by lictors (officers) bearing fasces (ceremonial axes), participate in a Senate meeting. Ancient Rome was divided into distinct social classes that narrowly defined one's prospects and destiny. At the bottom were the slaves, whose numbers and importance grew as Rome's military successes yielded ever more captives to be sold into bondage. On the next rung up were the *plebeians*, the craftspeople and manual laborers who retained their personal freedom. Above them stood the *equites* ("knights"), the commercial and trading classes. The highest social rank was the patrician class, the hereditary Roman nobility of families who claimed descent from the earliest Roman settlers or even from the gods; forbidden by law from engaging in trade, they amassed great fortunes from vast familial landholdings, the *latifundia* (see page 21).

Until Augustus, the Roman state had been a republic in which membership in the Senate was hereditary or appointive, while other key offices—including membership in the *Comitia Tributa*, the popular assembly of all citizens that voted on proposed laws—were filled through democratic election (slaves and women, however, could not vote). Among the important elective posts that defined the ladder of success for a young patrician politician were (in ascending order) the *quaestor* (there were eight; elected for one year) in charge of the state treasury; *aedile* (four; one year), equivalent to mayors; *tribune* (ten; elected by *Comitia Tributa*), guardians of plebeians' rights; *praetor* (six; two years), high judges; *censor* (two; eighteen months), supervised census-taking; *consul* (two; one year), chief executives of state, presided over Senate.

A praetor presiding over a trial. Roman law is perhaps that ancient culture's most important and enduring legacy. Basic ideas inherited from Rome are still at the heart of legal systems throughout the world, including our own. The Roman notion of natural law, which borrowed freely from the Greek tradition, appealed to rational rather than religious criteria. In Cicero's words, "True law is right reason consonant with nature, pervading all things, constant, eternal."

The idea of a universal law that stands above men was not meant to bind humanity but to liberate it from the caprice of tyranny; endlessly reinterpreted and refined, variously applied in the courts, Roman law was not a rigid, absolute system but an evolving ideal that was sometimes corrupted but never entirely abandoned in practice. Among the many Roman innovations that we now take for granted are the role of lawyers as professional advisers (although they were formally prohibited from taking fees, they were amply compensated with gifts and favors); trial by jury (adapted from the Greeks), composed of up to seventy-five citizens who decided criminal cases by majority vote; the right of women to own and inherit property; and the civil adjudication of contract disputes, including the right of appeal to a higher court.

Agricultural work on a large country estate (*latifundium*). From the time of the earliest kings to the Middle Republic, Italian agriculture was based on small holdings that produced mainly cereal crops and raised cattle in common pastures. As Rome expanded into the Mediterranean in the third to first centuries B.C., medium to large farms arose—typically 100 acres or so—and began to produce a wider variety of crops, with grapes and olives gradually overtaking grains, which were more cheaply obtainable from colonies in Sicily, Sardinia, Africa, and Asia Minor. As holdings grew larger during the late Republic and early Empire—roughly 100 B.C. to A.D. 100—cattle breeding and poultry raising became more important, along with the cultivation of a variety of fruits and vegetables.

Protracted stints in the army forced many citizen farmers to sell their land to wealthy patrician senators, who also augmented their holdings by laying claim to large tracts of the *ager publicus,* the vast government-owned territories acquired in war. The resulting huge estates—*latifundia*—were economically feasible because conquest also generated a flood of cheap labor in the form of slaves, some of whom worked under cruel and brutal conditions and were subjected to barbarous punishments for the smallest infractions; some were forced to work with their feet fettered or were chained to their cells at night. Other patricians, wishing to preserve the health of their labor force, provided their slaves with good food, decent quarters, and even amenities such as baths.

Leisure in a suburban (or seaside) villa. The original Latin word *villa* applied to a variety of dwellings: a small farmhouse, an elegant home in the country or suburbs, the lavish owner's quarters on a *latifundium*, or a seaside retreat. What they all shared was the traditional Roman concept of the *domus*, the patrician's house, which typically featured an *atrium*, an enclosed courtyard with a rectangular opening (*compluvium*) in the ceiling that let in rainwater to be collected directly below in a rectangular trough (*impluvium*) and drained away into a cistern in the basement. The *atrium* was the center of the house, variously a living room, dining room, and workroom. The entrances to additional rooms surrounded the *atrium*: the small bedrooms (*cubicola*); the *tablinum*, a large room typically serving as master bedroom or dining area; and, for the wealthiest, the *triclinium*, a

special dining room for elaborate feasting in the Greek reclining style. The largest villas were built around a *peristyle*, an open courtyard enclosed by a colonnade and often featuring elaborate gardens and sculpture.

Such elegance and style surrounded only a privileged few: of the fifty thousand buildings listed in the official record of Rome, only two thousand were patrician dwellings—most were *insulae*, the multistory tenements whose small, dark apartments housed the working class, sometimes adequately, sometimes appallingly, with overcrowded interiors bereft of light, heat, or plumbing (the nonpressurized Roman water supply was restricted to the ground floor); exposure to the noise and dirt of the streets; and frequent fires caused by torches and oil lamps used for lighting.

Banquet. Long before the wealth of empire fostered elaborate patrician feasts, there was the frugal table of the early Republic, a reflection of the spartan life of the citizen farmer and shepherd: the staple dish was porridge made of polenta meal, perhaps accompanied by spelt, legumes, and greens (bread later supplanted porridge). Meat and fish, for the most part, were luxuries reserved for special holiday feasts.

In the growing capital many of the manual laborers and artisans could afford a balanced if simple diet. But by 56 B.C. much of the swelling, impoverished proletariat of Rome required maintenance on a free dole of grain, their daily portion of which was typically their only meal of the day.

To the nobility, by contrast, the expanding empire brought riches and leisure and, from Greece and Asia, a taste for luxury and refine-

ment that liberated the patrician palate from its heritage of rustic parsimony. By the time of Tiberius (see page 12), the renowned gourmet Apicius had recorded 450 detailed epicurean recipes, many of which contain familiar elements: chicken, sausage, pork, fish, venison, honey, salt, pepper, olives, and garlic. But just as intriguing are the modern staples of which the Romans knew nothing: rice, potatoes, tomatoes, citrus fruits, sugar, coffee, tea, and chocolate.

Eventually no fashionable household was without a live-in kitchen staff, including a full-time chef charged with creating ever more outlandish delicacies for the all-night gastronomic orgies—complete with musicians and dancers—typical of Rome's nouveau riche (memorably satirized by Petronius in "Trimalchio's Feast" in his *Satyricon*). One writer reported a banquet of twenty-two courses, each accompanied by vintage wine!

A Roman military camp. Rome's growth into a vast empire was made possible by its advances in military organization and technique. During the continual foreign wars of the republican era, Rome did not maintain a standing army in the modern sense; troops and officers were prosperous citizen-soldiers recruited for specific military campaigns, even if this became, perforce, an annual procedure. Around 100 B.C., when the consul Marius introduced a volunteer system with longer periods of enrollment, the Roman forces began to evolve into a professional standing army capable of defending the growing empire. Drawn initially from the Italian peasantry and later in the Empire from the provincials as well, the legionary's chief loyalty was to his general and then to his pension and the spoils of war (which might include an eventual reward of land in conquered territory), incentives that often elicited a lifetime commitment to the army.

An instrument of superb mobility and tactical flexibility, the Roman army was divided into units of four to six thousand men called legions, each composed of ten cohorts, which were in turn subdivided into small mobile units of fifty to a hundred men called centuries, which were commanded by centurions. Arrayed two to three ranks deep in checkerboard formation, the intensively drilled legions, flanked by supporting cavalry and light infantry, overwhelmed enemy soldiers with wave upon wave of deadly spears and swords.

The legionary never knew an idle moment; when not training, engaged in battle, or hauling up to eighty pounds of equipment on extended marches, he was busy constructing elaborate fortified camps surrounded by ramparts and ditches. These bastions, unique to the Romans, were essential to holding vast stretches of conquered territory.

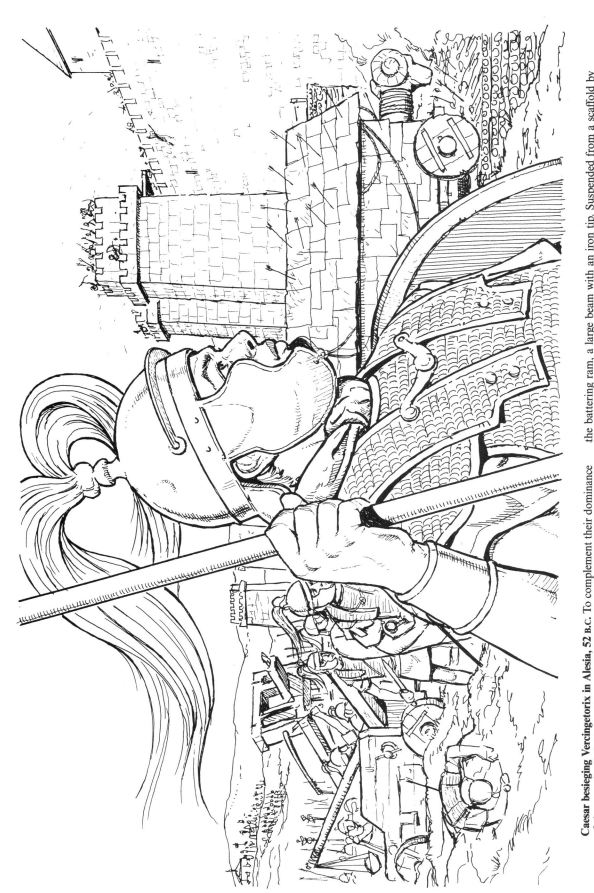

Caesar besieging Vercingetorix in Alesia, 52 B.C. To complement their dominance of the open battlefield, the Romans mastered siege warfare, the art of encircling, battering, and overrunning enemy fortresses. To this end they deployed an array of ingenious machines. The offensive devices included the *catapultae,* essentially large crossbows that fired light projectiles; *ballistae,* which could propel large stones or arrows at an angle over the enemy's walls; *scorpiones,* portable catapults; and the *onager,* a large catapult capable of hurling huge stones over 30 yards at heights of up to 40 yards. Among the protective devices were the *pluteus,* a rolling mantle covered with hide; the *testudo,* or "tortoise," a covered rolling platform that shielded soldiers while they undermined the foundation of enemy walls; the *vinae,* a series of wooden huts that allowed uninterrupted operation of the *aries,*

the battering ram, a large beam with an iron tip. Suspended from a scaffold by chains, the soldiers swung the *aries* forward to breach the enemy walls.

Siege techniques were critical in Caesar's conquest of Gaul, where his troops built an elaborate terrace of tree trunks—115 yards long, 16 yards wide, and 25 yards high—to surmount the walls at Avaricum. The highlight of the Gallic campaign, however, was Caesar's suppression of a revolt spearheaded by the chieftain Vercingetorix in 52 B.C. Trying to avoid open battle with Caesar's armies, the Gallic leader tried to resist the Romans from a few strongholds, one of which, Alesia, proved to be the site of the decisive battle; Caesar surrounded and besieged the tribal army holed up there, repulsed a relief effort by Gallic forces, and forced Vercingetorix's capitulation.

On the road. The world's first great highway system radiated from ancient Rome. It began in 312 B.C. with the Appian Way, which connected Rome to Capua; by the time of Trajan, the network had ramified to every corner of the vast empire: over fifty thousand miles of interconnecting arteries stretched from the Western tip of Spain to the eastern reaches of Asia Minor, abetting the flow of armies, goods, and ideas.

Marvels of engineering, the Roman highways always held to the straightest possible course, spanning lakes and rivers and cutting through mountains. Up to five yards wide and three feet deep, they were composed of several layers, or *strata:* a paved surface of gravel and stones was supported by tiers of stones and cement and a foundation of sand and chalk.

The carefully maintained roads served mainly official traffic, but private citizens could use them with special permission. Despite such conveniences as milestones (which marked the distance to Rome or the nearest provincial capital), posthouses (every ten miles), and inns (every thirty miles), life on the road could be harsh: merchants often joined armed convoys for fear of brigands; protection from the elements was minimal; and the inns were notoriously shabby, dangerous, and overpriced. Typical passenger conveyances included a two-wheeled chariot drawn by two to four horses and four-wheeled *raedae* (for freight or passengers) drawn by up to ten horses. Speeds varied widely: from fifteen miles per day to eighty miles per day for crack post riders and military vehicles.

Pont du Gard aqueduct near Nîmes, France. Rome's engineering genius was equally evident in its extensive system of aqueducts (from the Latin *aqua,* "water"; and *ductus,* "a leading" [from *ducere,* "to lead"]). Eleven of them, varying in length from 10 to 57 miles, were built over a period of five hundred years—from the third century B.C. to the second century A.D.—to carry water from the surrounding hills to cisterns in Rome.

Unlike modern pressure-driven water-distribution systems, the Roman aqueducts relied entirely on gravity. In each case the engineers were obliged to find the straightest possible path for a gradual downhill run that typically declined around 800 feet. Ensuring a steady flow across valleys and gorges sometimes meant constructing elevated arches that carried the water in a covered channel on the top tier. These

graceful architectural landmarks still adorn parts of Europe, most notably Nîmes, France (the Pont du Gard), and Segovia, Spain, where Trajan's arch, built some two thousand years ago, is still functioning, carrying water to the city from the Río Frío.

Because of their huge cost and limited applications, arches were only a small fraction of the total length of a typical Roman aqueduct: of the 260 miles of aqueducts entering Rome in the first century A.D., only 30 miles were atop arches. More typical were ground-level trenches (some of which were covered) and underground tunnels and pipes. Nearly half of the water from the aqueducts served the public (government buildings, baths, fountains, and public basins), about a third went to wealthy private parties, and the rest was reserved for the emperor.

The arch of Tiberius. The Romans' true genius lay in organization and engineering; for cultural inspiration they unabashedly and freely borrowed from Greece, in the visual arts no less than in literature, philosophy, and religion. In fact, throughout the late Republic and Empire, most of the leading artists and architects were Greek. The Hellenistic post-and-lintel approach to large-scale architecture was apparent in nearly all of Rome's major public buildings and temples.

The major architectural innovation of the Romans was the arch (the Greeks and Egyptians knew of the arch but did not feature it in their buildings), which not only lent a distinctive grace and beauty to Roman structures but also represented a technical advance, spanning large openings with easily portable stones

and bricks and providing better resistance to downward forces than the lintel. The key to the Romans' imposing arches was their development of higher grades of concrete able to withstand the outward stresses of the wedge-shaped blocks.

Long a central design feature of aqueducts and major public buildings such as the Colosseum, this elegant portal began to stand on its own in the form of triumphal arches, which were built to honor emperors or major military victories by generals. Usually placed along the route of the triumph, these monuments consisted of two piers supporting a central arch and an *attica*, or superstructure, that featured statues and reliefs; starting with Augustus, the large central arch was flanked by two smaller ones. Of the thirty-six triumphal arches once scattered throughout Rome, only three still stand.

Doctor with patient. Never formally regulated by the state, Roman medicine was a diverse affair, commingling in varying proportions magical-religious origins and scientific aspirations. Greek influences gradually dislodged the traditional Roman reliance on folk remedies and prayer; following a plague in 293 B.C., the Senate built a temple to the Greek god of medicine, Aesculapius, on a Tiber island. Although still steeped in sacrament, these early Greek inroads enhanced Roman receptivity to more scientific Hellenic approaches, especially those originating with Hippocrates, the fifth-century Greek physician whose ethical standards, diagnostic techniques, and theories became the point of departure for Roman medical science, at its best an earnest melange of empirical craft and herbal remedies, at its worst an invitation to free-lance charlatanry.

The social status of doctors varied widely in ancient Rome, where medicine remained largely a Greek franchise, with a sprinkling of Jews and Romans. Some rose to become wealthy *archiatri palatini*, physicians to the emperor and the aristocracy; others, the *archiatri populares*, were often freedmen who cared for farmers, urban workers, and the unemployed, sometimes in infirmaries (*valetudinaria*) built by the government, which also supported an impressive array of military hospitals and public works—aqueducts, sewers, and baths—that promoted general health.

Rome's most famous and influential doctors were the Greek-born Asclepiades (d. 40 B.C.), who challenged Hippocrates' naturopathic approach; his disciple Celsus, who codified his teachings in A.D. 30 in the book *De medicina;* and, preeminently, Galen, whose works remained the standard medical textbooks through the Middle Ages.

Schoolteacher with class. In the early years of the Republic, education was the responsibility of the family, especially the father, whose authority was absolute. Girls were trained in domestic tasks while the boys learned reading and the practical skills of managing an agricultural estate. Aside from the inculcation of the civic virtues that underlay the legal code, the general culture was narrowly religious, confined to worship of one's ancestors and the tribal gods.

With the conquest of Macedonia, Greece, and Pergamum in the second century B.C., the Romans climbed atop the shoulders of a superior Hellenistic culture. In the words of Horace, "Captive Greece captivated her rude conqueror and introduced the arts to rustic Latium." Educated Greek slaves served as teachers (*grammatici*) in private households and later in private schools, fostering an appreciation for

the Homeric epics—the bibles of Graeco-Roman culture—and, along with them, the Greek language, the acquisition of which became a requirement for Roman schoolboys.

In tightly disciplined classrooms (paddling was not uncommon), students wrote their lessons on *cerae* or *tabulae ceratae*, rectangular tablets spread with a thin layer of wax in which the student engraved letters with a sharpened wooden or metal rod (*stilus*). Books were papyrus scrolls with hand-copied text.

During the Empire the government became more active in supporting education, supplementing the schools of the *grammatici* with state-subsidized higher academies of rhetoric, philosophy, and law; nevertheless, distinguished young Roman scholars often pursued their higher learning in Greece.

31

Workshop manufacturing Arretine pottery. Throughout the Roman Empire a wide variety of preindustrial crafts and industries flourished: carpenters, flute makers, jewelers, dyers, leather workers, tanners, coppersmiths, and potters. Free artisans had long been organized into exclusive guilds (*collegia*), but in the last centuries of the Republic, Roman workshops relied heavily on slave labor; during the Empire free laborers became more common, and the state expanded the *collegia* to include both slaves and freedmen.

Among the most notable achievements of Roman craftsmanship was the glazed red pottery that emerged from the workshops of Arretium (today called Arezzo) and surrounding cities from 30 B.C. to A.D. 30. Unlike Greek vases, with their painted figures, the highly prized Arretine ware featured embossed patterns—trees, flowers, scenes from mythology and everyday life—formed from molds. Although most ancient artwork was anonymous, Arretine ware bears the stamped signatures of the factory owners and slaves who designed and manufactured the pieces.

The creation of a mosaic floor in a villa. Unlike Greek mosaics, which tended to ape the forms and patterns of wall paintings, Roman mosaics evolved into an original, distinctive art form. The original Greek mosaics made use of variously colored pebbles of similar size. Later Greek and early Roman craftsmen pioneered the use of *tesserae*, pieces cut to a uniform shape and size, in order to minimize visible patches of mortar and thereby create denser and more vivid images. Although stone remained in favor because of its durability in floor mosaics, the introduction of glass tesserae permitted a broader and brighter range of color.

Drawing on Hellenistic advances in mosaic technique from the conquered cities of Alexandria and Pergamum, Greek craftsmen in Roman Italy produced panoramas of stunning detail for the walls of public buildings and temples. A work found at Pompeii, which depicts the battle of Alexander and Darius at Issus, is the largest known mosaic and an example of the brilliantly dimensional detail possible in this medium.

Mosaics became increasingly popular for domestic decoration as well, as evidenced in the many tessellated floors preserved in the houses of Pompeii, which typically featured far simpler designs with little or no use of color. This rougher, more abstract style seemed better suited to the wear and tear of floors and household living, and gradually took hold as the prevailing aesthetic in the Hellenic eastern part of the Empire.

A sculptor working on a portrait bust. After the Roman conquests in Asia Minor, the burgeoning cultural influence of Greece registered powerfully in the art of sculpture as well. Even the earliest Roman sculpture bore traces of the Greek heritage by way of Etruscan influences, which, however, lacked the free-flowing refinement of Greek classicism. As the Empire expanded into the Hellenic east, that classic style, with its anatomical sophistication and graceful nobility of form, swept over the Roman world in the form of plunder and copies by Greek sculptors in Rome.

Not content merely to churn out pale derivations of Greek models, Roman sculptors scaled new artistic heights by breaking with Hellenic notions of the ideal and imparting a distinctively practical, hard-nosed Latin spirit to realistic portraiture of an order not rivaled before or since. This penetrating verisimilitude, which left an invaluable, unsparing record of the faces of ordinary citizens and great emperors alike, also infused the narrative reliefs so masterfully executed on various triumphal arches and the Column of Trajan, which still stands amidst the ruins of the Roman Forum.

Ostia, the port of Rome. By tradition a nation of farmers, Rome took to the sea more out of necessity than natural inclination. In an ever-widening empire, troops and goods could travel vast distances far more swiftly and efficiently by sea than on land. Having vanquished its chief Mediterannean rivals, Greece and Carthage, by emulating and surpassing their shipbuilding and seafaring techniques, Rome was now responsible for patrolling critical shipping routes (especially the grain shipments from Alexandria) and building a network of ports.

The Romans followed the Hellenic practice of constructing large, artificial ports that could be buttressed against waves and erosion. The most notable example was at Ostia, Rome's only major port until the early Empire, when Claudius built a large artificial harbor there to handle the spiraling volume of trade; fifty years later, in A.D. 103, the harbor was expanded by Trajan. Observing the scene at Ostia, an observer wrote: "The arrival and departure of ships never stops—it is amazing that the sea, not to mention the harbor, is big enough for these merchant ships."

The typical Roman cargo ship had a wooden hull, measured 30 to 96 yards in length, could hold 110 to 180 tons, and had a gross tonnage of 250 to 300. A large central mast carried the main sail, while a smaller sail attached to the foremast. Only in windless conditions did cargo ships rely on oarsmen, the chief means of propulsion for Roman warships.

A street of open shops of all types. Much of our knowledge of commercial street life in ancient Rome and environs comes from the extensive ruins of Pompeii, the prosperous coastal town that was buried by a deadly eruption of Mount Vesuvius in A.D. 79 and thus preserved in museumlike detail until excavated by archaeologists nearly two thousand years later (see pages 16 and 17).

Many of the residences in Pompeii seem to have been fronted by small shops that opened onto the street. To the rear of each shop was a small apartment, in some cases with upstairs sleeping quarters. The vanished life of this ancient sidewalk seems almost to breathe again in the myriad remnants: trinkets from the silversmith, fruits preserved in glass containers, fishing nets, bread molds and bread loaves in a bakery, a surgeon's bronze instruments, the tools of a blacksmith, a sculptor's implements alongside half-finished blocks of marble. There are

also dyers' shops, a tannery, a fullery, a lamp factory, wine and food shops, and even the local headquarters of the world's oldest profession. The stone-paved streets, deeply rutted from the wheels of carts, feature sidewalks and stepping stones to raise pedestrians above the wet, dirty surface. As in contemporary cities, the walls are full of graffiti that speak of love (sometimes none too delicately), loss, and politics.

A busy port town, Pompeii also furnished ample means of rest and diversion to the weary traveler, with taverns and inns dotting the city gates and forum. The more elegant restaurants served reclining patrons in a garden; in the cheaper establishments customers ate on stools in a small, dark room.

A *suovetaurilia.* Despite Augustus's efforts to systematize Roman religious beliefs into an official state doctrine that would help to undergird imperial authority, the religion of Rome remained what it had always been: a meandering, polytheistic current fed by streams of traditional agrarian nature-god worship and periodic freshets flowing from the east—initially from Greece in the form of Olympian mythology, and later from Egypt, Judaea, and Asia Minor in the form of orgiastic Bacchic cults, Isis worship, Mithraism, and Christianity.

The Roman pantheon arose from a sturdy foundation of peasant animism largely devoid of spiritual or ethical content, a religion in which the very root word, *religare*—"to bind"—bespeaks the dryly contractual nature of the relationship between humans and the gods. *Do ut es* ("I give so that you may give") was a defining tenet of early Roman worship, which involved closely specified rituals of prayer and sacrifice to the gods in exchange for the blessings of earthly health and prosperity. One such rite was the *suovetaurilia,* the sacrifice of a pig, sheep, or bull in which the internal organs were offered to the gods and the remainder reserved for human consumption at the ensuing banquet. Some sacrifices were overseen by a *haruspex,* a specialist in discerning divine portents in animal entrails.

Vestal virgins tending the sacred fire. Vesta, one of the earliest and most enduring of the Roman deities, was the goddess of the hearth, which symbolized the sanctity of the home and the family. The sacred hearth flame sustained each household, cooking its food and warding off the chill and darkness of the night. Every community kept a public symbolic hearth fire tended by the only true priestesses of ancient Roman culture, the *Virgines vestales* (vestal virgins), whose prayers were deemed essential to the general welfare. During the imperial epoch, six vestal virgins tended an eternally burning flame—the symbol of Rome's imperial destiny—in a round temple in the Forum under the authority of the *pontifex maximus.* (This was Rome's most venerable pagan tradition, lasting until the flame was finally extinguished in A.D. 382, during the Christian era.)

Believed to possess unearthly powers tied to their virginity, these maidens were accorded sacred status: a convicted criminal who happened to cross their path was to be freed immediately. But any wavering from their exalted calling exacted a horrible toll: if a virgin allowed the eternal flame to die out, she was severely beaten; if she lost her virginity, she was buried alive.

Funeral of a wealthy nobleman; people carrying images of his ancestors. Lacking any theological tradition tying earthly conduct to the soul's otherworldly fate, mainstream Roman religion did not dwell much on death and the afterlife. For Romans death was not a prelude to divine reward or punishment; the soul joined the *Manes* (pure, good spirits), passing into a state of pure holiness that graced the sepulcher, which was considered a holy place.

For the first seven days the corpse lay in the *atrium* of the house, where the female family members wailed in ritual lamentation, shouting the name of the deceased in the hope of calling back his soul from the dead. After this week of mourning, the body was carried to a site outside the city walls in a parade con-

sisting of musicians, torch-bearers, hired mourners (who sang traditional dirges), and, in the case of distinguished noblemen, a procession of masked actors representing the ancestors of the dead man; his accomplishments were cited on placards. After ritual burning of the corpse at the funeral pyre, the relatives washed the remains and sealed them in an urn that was placed inside a monument. The tomb, often an altar, bore inscriptions to the deceased and was sometimes the site of ceremonial sacrifices. Great importance was placed on wrapping the corpse in a winding-sheet; failure to do so required the sacrifice of a sow in expiation.

Even ordinary citizens, though buried with far less pomp, had funeral monuments. Slaves were usually buried in a mass grave.

Worship of Mithra, with typical Mithraic altar. The official Roman religion, with its stress on loyalty to the state, ancient tradition, and worldly success, left a spiritual and moral void that was filled increasingly by the mystery religions emanating from the Hellenic east. Among these, the most serious competitor of Christianity was Mithraism, an Indo-Persian cult devoted to Mithra, the god of light.

Most of the Roman Mithraic chapels (*spelaea*) were actual caves that accommodated fifty to a hundred worshipers who could sit or kneel before a centerpiece depicting Mithra's slaying of the sacred bull, whose seed generated all life, an event so central to the Mithraic creation myth that initiates were often bathed in the blood of a freshly killed bull.

Combining the allure of secrecy with a bracing moral code and the prospect of spiritual transformation, Mithraism, an exclusively male sect, attracted adherents among all classes—aristocrats, freedmen, soldiers, and the poor—who worshiped shoulder to shoulder in the grottoes. It is unclear to what extent Mithraists merely complemented or entirely abandoned their traditional Roman paganism, but inscriptions to Mithra begin to appear in ruins dating from 136 B.C. and thenceforth proliferate rapidly. Because of Mithra's popularity among the legions, his name frequently appears in inscriptions to soldiers of all ranks, and Mithraic altars and sanctuaries have been found throughout the northern and eastern military outposts of the Empire. Dedications to Mithra seem to vanish abruptly from the record in the fourth century, when Christianity, another eastern import, became the official state religion.

Christians worshiping secretly in a private home. When Romans began searching for alternatives to the state-sponsored paganism, the very roads and sea lanes that had helped to spread traditional Roman culture now helped to undermine it, as new religious influences flowed to the heart of the Empire from points east.

Thirsting for a sense of wholeness amidst their polyglot of traditional deities, many Romans grew receptive to monotheism, an idea spread chiefly by the Jews, who constituted 10 percent of the population of the Empire by the time of Nero. Christianity, initially an offshoot of Judaism, burgeoned into a vigorous new religious movement that was at first tolerated as a Jewish sect. But as it won numerous converts, Christianity, which rejected animal sacrifices to the emperor and openly disparaged the traditional pagan gods, appeared to threaten the underpinnings of imperial authority. Falsely accused of barbarous secret rites and seditious plots, Christians were subjected to numerous waves of persecution, beginning with Nero in A.D. 64 (although more recent scholarship has questioned the reality of Nero's persecution) and continuing sporadically for the next 250 years.

Surmounting these adversities, Christianity spread rapidly throughout the Empire, winning an edict of toleration in 313 from the emperor Constantine, who had converted to Christianity the year before. Until the fourth century most Christians had worshiped in private homes, but now many pagan temples were converted into churches. Christianity became the official state religion of the Roman Empire in 392.

Children at play. Knowledge of children's games in ancient Rome comes largely from archaeological sources. Clay dolls were popular among young girls, who enjoyed running imaginary households. Frescoes show children playing a game with sticks, the rules of which are unknown. Little carts were also a favorite diversion; sometimes children attached mice to them and held miniature chariot races. Knuckle bones tossed in the air served for a game similar to dice. A popular party game was "copper fly," a version of blind man's bluff in which a child wearing a blindfold cried, "I'll catch the copper fly!" while being taunted with shouts and sticks by playmates. Older boys enjoyed fierce athletic competition, which formed part of their early military training.

Chariot race in the Circus Maximus. "The people that once bestowed commands, consulships, legions, and all else, now meddles no more and longs eagerly for just two things—bread and circuses." Thus did the writer Juvenal portray the Roman passion for the dramatic, often bloody spectacles of the circus and amphitheater.

The largest and most famous arena was the Circus Maximus, where chariot drivers raced for riches and glory before 250,000 roaring enthusiasts. A combination of ancient rite, social event, carnival, gambling den, and ferocious competition, the chariot race began with the *pompa circensis,* a ritual parade featuring the chief magistrate, the competitors, effigies of the gods, musicians, dancers, and satyrs. At the starting signal the helmeted charioteers, guiding two to four horses, took off in two-wheeled, wooden boxes kept in balance only by the driver's nerve and agility. Straining and careering through seven laps of the crowded 840-yard course, the drivers courted death at every turn, quickening the pulse of the ravening throng. Although some drivers earned enduring fame and unimaginable wealth by accumulating hundreds or even thousands of victories, many were cut down in their prime. The survivors were heroes, revered by the masses, indulged by the police, and courted by beautiful women.

Gladiators fight to the death. The brutal streak in the Roman sensibility was even better served by gladiatorial fighting, which guaranteed the fatal outcome that the circus races provided only fitfully. Originating in the early Republic as a funeral rite, perhaps a remnant of the Samnite practice of human sacrifice at the tombs of the wealthy, these mortal combats gradually shed their sacred origins and became a mass entertainment devoid of any purpose but slaking the spectators' vicarious thirst for blood.

Drawn mostly from the ranks of prisoners of war, slaves, and criminals, the future fighters were sent to gladiatorial schools for intensive training before being thrust into armed battles to the death before thousands of spectators in amphitheaters such as the Colosseum in Rome (see page 18). Pliny the younger, seeking a toehold in virtue for this ritual carnage, wrote that the arena clashes "lit the flame of courage by showing that the love of glory and the desire to win could be found even in the hearts of slaves and criminals."

These "games" came in several varieties: the *venationes* were displays of exotic wild animals, often pitted against each other or against an armed or unarmed gladiator (much like the modern bullfight); the centerpiece was the struggle between two armed gladiators who fought until mutual exhaustion, until one slew the other, or until one raised his hand in surrender. If the loser fought well, the crowd might shout "*Mitte!*" (let him go); if the horde judged him a coward, they shouted "*Jugula!*" (cut his throat), and the losing gladiator was obliged to expose his throat for the death blow.

Roman baths. Yet another borrowing from the Greeks, who bathed after their exercises in the gymnasium, the Roman bath (*therma*) evolved from modest beginnings in the Republic, first in the form of simple wash houses in private homes and later in small public baths run by entrepreneurs. In the first century A.D. the emperors greatly expanded bath facilities as a public benefaction: in 33 B.C. Rome had 170 *thermae;* at the height of the empire there were a thousand, with hundreds more scattered throughout the Empire. Agrippa, Augustus's chief advisor, built public baths that were free to all so that the poorest laborer might find himself sweating alongside a senator in the steam room. To meet the growing demand, later emperors built ever larger and more lavish facilities: Diocletian's baths occupied thirty-two acres and Caracalla's thirty-three, each of them serving five thousand customers per day and requiring a staff of ten thousand. Libraries (Greek and Latin), meeting rooms, restaurants, gardens, courtyards—even rooms for prostitutes—complemented the bathing and exercise facilities in these cities within a city. (Women bathed at special hours or in separate bathhouses.)

A typical visit might begin with a rubdown with oil in the *unctorium,* followed by a hot, steaming bath in the *caldarium* and a spell of dry heat in the *laconium* (sauna). Having sweated out the dirt, the bather might scrape his skin clean with a curved, bronze *strigil.* After cooling off in the warm *tepidarium,* the Roman would end his routine with a bracing splash in the *frigidarium,* the cold pool.

Actors performing in a Roman theater. Like the races and the gladiatorial combats, the Roman theater was a secular diversion with roots in sacred Etruscan funeral rites. But unlike the circus and arena, which bore an original if brutish Roman trademark, the theater remained a Greek derivative, relying mainly on reworkings of the Hellenic repertory. With its emphasis on attracting a mass audience (the Theater of Marcellus had a capacity of twenty thousand), the Roman theater lavished most of its energy on spectacular sets, elaborate choreography, and promoting star worship of the leading actors, whose faces were well known to the public, Greek-style masks having gradually fallen out of fashion.

Even though slaves and criminals were occasionally brought on stage to suffer in real life the executions called for by the plot, the the-ater was hard pressed to compete with the blood-drenched spectacles of the amphitheater and circus; it was allotted far fewer festival days (forty-five under Augustus, compared to a hundred or more for races and fighting), and performances usually took place in the morning to avoid conflict with the far more popular games.

It was in the last two centuries of the Republic that Rome produced its only playwrights of real distinction: Gnaeus Naevius (c. 270–c. 200 B.C.), who pioneered the *fabula togata* (comedy with a Roman subject) and *fabula praetexta* (Roman historical tragedy); Plautus (254–184 B.C.), considered by some the West's first great comic playwright; and Terence (c. 186–c. 159 B.C.), who based most of his plays on the works of the Greek playwright Menander.

Vergil reading aloud to a group of friends from the *Aeneid*. Augustus's reign ushered in a golden age not only in statecraft but also in literature and general culture. His patrician adviser Maecenas served as patron to the leading poets of the age, seeking to gather their talents into a national literature that would impart a glow of spiritual destiny to Rome's imperial ambitions. This project was admirably served by Vergil (70–19 B.C.), a poet from rustic Mantua who became, through Maecenas's patronage, a confidant of Augustus and the author of the *Aeneid,* the epic poem that chronicles Italy's saga from its founding by Aeneas of Troy through Rome's march to imperial power, which Vergil portrays not as selfish conquest but as the fulfillment of the gods' will that earthly dominion should belong to the righteous and just.

Was the poet seated too near the emperor's throne to see the brutality that underlay the splendor? Is it perhaps true, as Emerson wrote, that "the barbarians who broke up the Roman empire did not arrive a day too soon"? To be sure, contradictions leap off every page of Roman history: the abysmal cruelty of its arenas and the soaring grace of its temples, the excesses of its emperors and the eloquence of its lawmakers, the ugliness of its slavery and the beauty of its poetry, the blight of its wars and the benefactions of its roads and aqueducts. Yet even though buffeted by savage tempests, the vestal flame, the noble symbol of Rome's civilizing mission, burned for nearly a thousand years.